Little Ducks Go

Little Ducks Go

by Emily Arnold McCully

Holiday House / New York

Copyright © 2014 by Emily Arnold McCully
All Rights Reserved
HOLIDAY HOUSE is registered in the U.S. Patent and Trademark Office.
Printed and Bound in October 2014 at Tien Wah Press, Johor Bahru, Johor, Malaysia.
The artwork was created with pen and ink and watercolors.
www.holidayhouse.com
3 5 7 9 10 8 6 4 2

Library of Congress Cataloging-in-Publication Data
McCully, Emily Arnold, author, illustrator.
Little ducks go / by Emily Arnold McCully. — First edition.
pages cm. — (I like to read)
Summary: Mother Duck is on the run trying
to keep her ducklings safe.
ISBN 978-0-8234-2941-7 (hardcover)
[1. Ducks—Fiction.
2. Animals—Infancy—Fiction.]
I. Title.
PZ7.M478415Lhm 2014
[E]—dc23
2013009559

ISBN 978-0-8234-3300-1 (paperback)

Little ducks go.

Look out, little ducks!

Little ducks go.

They go down.

Mother looks down.

"Quack," she says.

Little ducks look up.

"Cheep cheep," they say.

Little ducks go.

Mother runs.

Mother looks down.

"Quack!"

Little ducks look up.

"Cheep cheep!"

Little ducks go.

Mother runs.

Cars come.

Look out!

She is safe.

Mother runs.

Little ducks go.

"Cheep cheep!"

Little ducks stop.

Mother stops too.

She wants help.

But the man goes away.

Mother looks down.

"Quack," she says.

"Cheep cheep," she hears.

She sits.

The man comes back.

Little ducks get into the net.

They are safe!

Little ducks go home.
"Cheep cheep cheep
cheep cheep cheep!"
"Quack!"

You will like these too!

The Big Fib by Tim Hamilton

Dinosaurs Don't, Dinosaurs Do
by Steve Björkman

Fish Had a Wish by Michael Garland
Kirkus Reviews Best Children's Books list
and Top 25 Children's Books list

I Said, "Bed!" by Bruce Degen

I Will Try by Marilyn Janovitz

Look! by Ted Lewin

Pete Won't Eat by Emily Arnold McCully

See Me Run by Paul Meisel
A Theodor Seuss Geisel Award Honor Book

See more I Like to Read books.
Go to www.holidayhouse.com/I-Like-to-Read/

I Like to Read® Books in Paperback
You will like all of them!

Bad Dog by David McPhail

The Big Fib by Tim Hamilton

Boy, Bird, and Dog by David McPhail

Can You See Me? by Ted Lewin

Car Goes Far by Michael Garland

Come Back, Ben by Ann Hassett and John Hassett

The Cowboy by Hildegard Müller

Dinosaurs Don't, Dinosaurs Do by Steve Björkman

Ed and Kip by Kay Chorao

The End of the Rainbow by Liza Donnelly

Fireman Fred by Lynn Rowe Reed

Fish Had a Wish by Michael Garland

The Fly Flew In by David Catrow

Good Night, Knight by Betsy Lewin

Grace by Kate Parkinson

Happy Cat by Steve Henry

I Have a Garden by Bob Barner

I Said, "Bed!" by Bruce Degen

I Will Try by Marilyn Janovitz

Late Nate in a Race by Emily Arnold McCully

The Lion and the Mice by Rebecca Emberley and Ed Emberley

Little Ducks Go by Emily Arnold McCully

Look! by Ted Lewin

Look Out, Mouse! by Steve Björkman

Me Too! by Valeri Gorbachev

Mice on Ice by Rebecca Emberley and Ed Emberley

Pete Won't Eat by Emily Arnold McCully

Pig Has a Plan by Ethan Long

Ping Wants to Play by Adam Gudeon

Sam and the Big Kids by Emily Arnold McCully

See Me Dig by Paul Meisel

See Me Run by Paul Meisel
A THEODOR SEUSS GEISEL AWARD HONOR BOOK

Sick Day by David McPhail

3, 2, 1, Go! by Emily Arnold McCully

What Am I? Where Am I? by Ted Lewin

You Can Do It! by Betsy Lewin

Visit http://www.holidayhouse.com/I-Like-to-Read/ for more about I Like to Read® books, including flash cards, reproducibles, and the complete list of titles.